How To Be A SUPERCOW!

Deborah Fajerman

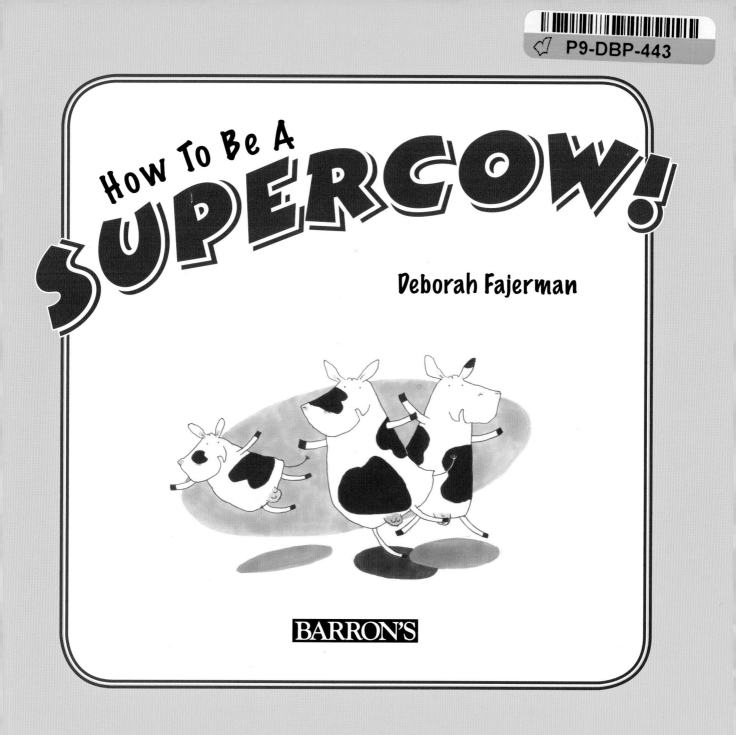

BARRON'S

It's the end of the day. The little cows are tired, and Mommy Cow says, *"Time for bed!"*

But when they hear those words,
the little cows jump up and whisper:

SHUSSSSSSHHHHHHHHHHHHHHHHHHHHHHHH!

Although we look like normal, average little cows,

we're actually, secretly…

Super

Yes, we are in the secret
supercow crew.

cows!

We just can't go to bed,
we have too much to do.

Like rescue a dragon from an angry princess.

Then put out the fire,

and clean up the mess.

We can catch pirates,
and rescue the gold.

We march all our prisoners
down to the hold.

They'll never escape, 'cause we tied them up tight.
Though we're not really sure if we did the knots right.

We can show you the way if you're new in town.

Though sometimes we might read the map upside down.

We're always quite brave,
and we never fear our foes,

 like creepy-crawlies,   carrots,

and a kiss on the nose.

You can call for our help if you're stuck in a flood.

(But you may end up smelly and covered in mud.)

We'll fix the trouble if your tractor won't start:
we'll push it, and poke it, and take it apart.

We help all our friends
to fasten their laces.

We help babies have naps
when we make funny faces.

It once was a secret
but now it's been said:
we are all supercows

AND WE WON'T GO TO BED!

You really are supercows! I'd never have guessed.
But you can't do your job if you're improperly dressed.

You'll need the right costume, otherwise how will people know you're a supercow?

If your teeth are nice and shiny, it helps you see at night.

And if you wash your faces, you're sure to get things right.

YawwwwwnNNnnnnn

Maybe even supercows do need to go to bed.
We can do all that other stuff tomorrow instead.

Z z z

Sleep well, little ones.
Kiss, kiss, kiss, hushabye.

When you wake up...

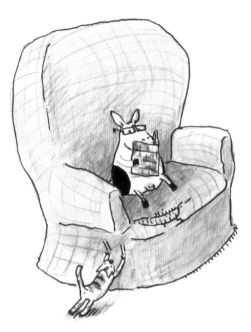

To Sylvia and Rose: Supercows!

First edition for the United States and Canada published in 2018
by Barron's Educational Series, Inc.

Copyright © 2018 by Deborah Fajerman

All inquiries should be addressed to:
Barron's Educational Series, Inc.
250 Wireless Boulevard
Hauppauge, New York 11788
www.barronseduc.com

ISBN: 978-1-4380-1158-5

Library of Congress Control Number: 2018934186

Date of Manufacture: July 2018
Manufactured by: L08E08O, Heshan City, Guangdong, China

Printed in China

9 8 7 6 5 4 3 2 1